MELOWY

The Ice Enchantment

Danielle Star

Scholastic Inc.

Published by Scholastic Inc., *Publishers since 1920,*
557 Broadway, New York, NY 10012. SCHOLASTIC and associated logos are trademarks and/or registered trademarks of Scholastic Inc.

ISBN 978-1-338-15180-0

Text by Danielle Star
Original title *L'incanto del ghiaccio*
Editorial cooperation by Lucia Vaccarino
Illustrations by Emilio Urbano (layout), Roberta Tedeschi (cleanup), and Patrizia Zangrilli (colors)
Graphics by Danielle Stern

Special thanks to Tiffany Colón
Translated by Chris Turner
Interior design by Baily Crawford

10 9 8 7 6 5 4 3 2 1   18 19 20 21 22

Printed in the U.S.A.   40
First printing 2018

Contents

1. A Magical Morning

1

2. The Art of Powers Teachers

9

3. The Adventure Begins!

17

4. An Icy Beginning

27

5. A Visit Home

37

6. Rainbow Milk Shakes

49

7. The Forbidden Book

59

8. Cleo's Power

69

Imagine a magical land wrapped in golden light. A planet in a distant galaxy beyond the known stars. This enchanted place is known as Aura, and it is very special. For Aura is home to the pegasus, a winged horse with a colorful mane and coat.

The pegasuses of Aura come from four ancient island realms that lie within Aura's enchanted oceans: the Winter Realm of Amethyst Island, the Spring Realm of Emerald Island, the Day Realm of Ruby Island, and the Night Realm of Sapphire Island.

A selected number from each realm are born with a symbol on their wings and a hidden magical power. These are the Melowies.

When their magic beckons them in a dream, all Melowies leave their island homes to answer the call. They must attend school at the Castle of Destiny, a legendary castle hidden in a sea of clouds, where they will learn all about their hidden powers. Destiny is a place where friendships are born, where Melowies find their courage, and where they discover the true magic inside themselves!

The Day Realm

Castle of Destiny

The Night Realm

Map of the Castle of Destiny

1 Butterfly Tower—first-year dormitory

2 Dragonfly Tower—second-year dormitory

3 Swallow Tower—third-year dormitory

4 Eagle Tower—fourth-year dormitory

5 Principal Gia's office

6 Library

7 Classrooms

8 The Winter Tower

9 The Spring Tower

10 The Day Tower

11 The Night Tower

12 Waterfall

13 Runway

14 Assembly hall

15 Garden

16 Sports fields

17 Cafeteria

18 Kitchen

19 Auditorium

Meet the Melowies

Cleo

Her realm: unknown
Her personality: impulsive and loyal
Her passion: writing
Her gift: something mysterious . . .

Electra

Her realm: Day
Her personality: boisterous and bubbly
Her passion: fashion
Her gift: the Power of Light

Maya

Her realm: Spring
Her personality: shy and sweet
Her passion: cooking
Her gift: the Power of Heat

Cora

Her realm: Winter
Her personality: proud and sincere
Her passion: ice-skating
Her gift: the Power of Cold

Selena

Her realm: Night
Her personality: deep and sensitive
Her passion: music
Her gift: the Power of Darkness

1
A Magical Morning

It was a beautiful, warm morning at the Castle of Destiny. The gentle breeze blowing off the sea of clouds made the air fresh and fragrant. It was an excellent start to a new day.

"Ew!" Maya cried. Her usually perfect mane was a complete mess. It was time to get out of bed, but she still had her blanket pulled right up to her nose.

"What are you ewwing about?" asked Cora, who was always up first. She was already dressed and her mane was styled beautifully.

"Today is our first Art of Powers class," Maya groaned, burying herself even deeper under the covers. "Don't tell me you've forgotten."

"Of course I haven't forgotten!" cried Cora. "I'm so excited. I can hardly wait for it to start!"

Love It (handwritten)

"Lucky you. I'm terrified!" Maya muttered, finally sitting up in bed. "I'm so nervous that I didn't sleep at all last night."

Selena groaned and stretched. She hadn't slept very well, either.

Art of Powers class was very important for Melowies. Not only because it was something they had been dreaming about since they were little fillies, but also because they couldn't become true Melowies unless they learned to use their powers properly. Getting a bad grade in Art of Powers meant being expelled from the Castle of Destiny.

Electra yawned loudly. She had slept like a log and had only just woken up. She lay with her head hanging off the side of the bed, and her tail rested on her pillow.

"You'd better get a move on, sleepyhead," cried Cora. "You don't want to be late today!"

"Why? What is so special about today?" Electra mumbled, rubbing sleep out of her eyes.

"It's the first day of Art of Powers class," sighed Selena. "As if we don't have enough schoolwork already . . . I still haven't gotten over our survival challenge in the Neon Forest."

"But we all did really well!" said Electra. "Even though I went off after that egg. This class is going to be great. I can feel it. I already know how to use my power a little. I realized that the other day." Electra winked at her friends and concentrated hard. Her face turned orange and was hot to the touch. Melowies from the Day Realm, like her, were connected with the sun's energy and light.

"Are you sure you know what you're doing?" Selena asked. "You look like you're going to burst into flames."

Electra was getting hotter and hotter. Sparks started to fly off her mane.

"No problem! Everything is fine! Don't panic . . . but I can't seem to stop it!" Electra cried, waving her arms to cool herself down.

Cora rushed out of the room and came back a moment later with a bucket of water.

Splash!

She threw the water at Electra, soaking her entire mane. Things stopped heating up as Maya and Selena laughed and laughed.

"Thank you!" Electra snapped, annoyed.

"Thanks so much, Cora. You really know how to help out a friend."

Maya stopped laughing. "Speaking of friends, has anyone seen Cleo?"

They all flew over to Cleo's bed and looked under the pile of blankets. The bed was empty.

2
The Art of Powers Teachers

Cleo had woken up before everyone else and quietly left their room in Butterfly Tower. She was worried, and she knew a solo flight was the only way to clear her head.

All the students were nervous to start Art of Powers classes, but Cleo was even more nervous than the rest of them. When she was a baby, the principal of the Castle of Destiny had found her on the front steps of the school. Cleo had been raised there and had no idea what realm she was from or what her power was.

Hovering over the clouds with her pink mane flowing in the wind, she saw some of the other students below starting to make their way to class.

"Hey, Cleo!" cried Melanie, a lemon-yellow Melowy.

"Hi, Cleo!" called Lycia, a purple Melowy.

"Hello," Cleo called back, and followed them quietly to the school's main entrance.

"I'm so nervous!" Lycia exclaimed.

"Me, too!" said Melanie. "I wonder what the teacher will be like."

Cleo sighed. As they walked toward the stairs, she saw a whole lot of nervous

Melowies, but she felt different from all of them. She felt unique, and not in a good way.

At least they all knew where they came from.

"There she is!" cried Electra from across the hall. "Where did you disappear to?"

"The first class is in the assembly hall," said Maya. The friends all walked together.

The assembly hall was on the second floor of the castle's main tower. The students all looked a little scared as they walked in. After their Defense Techniques class with the terrifying Ms. Ariadne, they couldn't imagine what their Art of Powers teacher, Mr. Zelus, would be like.

"I bet he will be a big and scary Megas!" Selena whispered with a shudder as she entered the hall with her friends.

There were rows of padded stools surrounding a stage in the middle of the room. The ceiling above them had paintings of scenes from the history of Aura.

"What if he is even worse than Ms. Ariadne?" Maya wondered aloud as she sat down.

A buzz of nervous whispers and giggles filled the room. Even Eris didn't seem as smug as she usually was. Neither did the two new friends she had been spending all her time with lately, Leda and Kate. Leda was laughing nervously, and Kate's face was tight with worry.

"I think he will be tall with fiery eyes and enormous wings," Electra whispered, beating her own wings together dramatically.

"Hey, look out!" Cora growled with a glare when one wing whacked her. Just then, she noticed that everyone else in the hall had fallen silent.

Cora and Electra looked up, expecting to see the scariest teacher ever. Instead, they saw an elderly, skinny Megas. His mane was thinning and had lots of wrinkles. He was wearing a woolen cardigan that was too big for his small frame. "Ahem. Good morning, girls. I am Mr. Zelus, and I teach Art of

Powers." He noticed that the Melowies were staring at him and took the opportunity to surprise them a little bit more by creating a lovely snowfall with his wings.

"Wow!" all of the Melowies exclaimed at once.

"As you may have been able to guess, I am from the Winter Realm. My three colleagues and I will be teaching you how to use your powers. Ms. Iris, Mr. Hector, and Ms. Diane, please step forward. We will all be your Art of Powers teachers, one from each realm."

Ms. Iris, a Melowy from the Spring Realm,

had a flowing green mane and a sincere smile. Mr. Hector, from the Night Realm, was a jolly Megas with a purple coat. Ms. Diane, from the Day Realm, was a slender Melowy with a beautiful golden coat.

"Please follow me to the middle of the hall," Mr. Zelus continued. "Divide yourselves into realms behind your teachers." Everyone stood up and quickly organized themselves into the four groups. Everyone except Cleo.

3

The Adventure Begins!

"Good morning, Cleo," Mr. Zelus said, tilting his head slightly to one side. "I used to catch you spying on classes now and then when you were younger. I am so happy to see that you are finally in one!"

"Umm . . . good morning, sir," Cleo mumbled. She could feel the eyes of all the other first-year students on her. Standing behind Mr. Zelus, Eris, Kate, and Leda were pointing at her and giggling. "What should

I do?" Cleo asked nervously, feeling very embarrassed.

"Oh, that's easy," said Ms. Iris with a smile. "You'll just have to do a little more work than the other girls."

"More work?"

"Yes, but you will soon see that it will be worth it."

Mr. Zelus, who was a little distracted, agreed. "Yes, like last time . . . with that other student."

"Other student? Do you mean there was another student like me?" Cleo asked excitedly. "A student with no realm? Can I talk to her?"

Mr. Hector shared a discreet glance with Mr. Zelus, who quickly coughed and straightened up. "What's that, Cleo? No, you can't talk to her. She isn't here anymore."

Mr. Hector quickly changed the subject. "Everyone, please line up behind your teacher now."

The students all formed lines behind the teachers from their realms, with Cleo bringing up the rear. Her heart was pounding. So, she wasn't the only Melowy with no realm after all! But what on earth would she have to do now?

The teachers led the Melowies upstairs and into a round room with four doors. Above each door there was a symbol: a sun, a flower, a star, and a snowflake. "This is where we will part ways," announced Mr. Zelus. "These doors lead to the tower of each realm. That is where you will each learn to use your power."

Each teacher opened a door, and the students all looked through, wide-eyed and amazed. The Spring Tower had grass in place of a floor and lush vines with gorgeous flowers covering all the walls. The Day Tower was warm, and a smell of summer air drifted through the open door. The Night Tower was all blue. Its vaulted ceilings were speckled with stars, and the Melowies could hear the chirping of crickets in the distance. The Winter Tower was as chilly as a December morning, with huge chandeliers made of snowflake-shaped crystals hanging from the ceiling.

"Classes will be held here one afternoon a week," Mr. Zelus said. "Winter Realm students, who are lucky enough to have me as their teacher, will attend class on Mondays. Tuesdays, Day Realm students will be with Ms. Diane. Wednesdays you will have free.

Thursdays, Ms. Iris will teach the Melowies from the Spring Realm, and on Fridays, Mr. Hector will teach the Night Realm students."

"What should I do?" Cleo asked.

"You will attend all the classes. That's the only way we will be able to find out the nature of your power and which realm you are from."

That afternoon, Cleo and Cora went to their first Art of Powers class. "I d-d-don't think I'm r-r-right for the Winter Realm." Cleo's teeth were chattering after just five minutes in the icy Winter Tower.

"You aren't cold, are you?" Cora looked at her in amazement. "This is the perfect temperature! Don't you feel totally energized?!"

"Well, look who we have here," came a familiar, cold voice.

"Eris!" exclaimed Cleo, but that was all she could say. The cold had frozen her ability to crack jokes! Luckily, Eris's friends Leda and Kate weren't there since they were from the Spring and Day Realms.

"I am from the Winter Kingdom, so I feel at home here," Eris continued. "You, on the other hand . . . Well, you should get ready to look like a real fool, Cleo."

"You *are* the expert in that, Eris," growled Cora.

The other Melowy shook her mane angrily. "Listen, Miss Prissy, you better get ready to lose your place as first in the class."

"Enough chatter, students," announced Mr. Zelus as he came into the classroom. "Everyone gather around. One of the most exciting adventures of your lives is about to begin!"

4
An Icy Beginning

Cleo took a look around the room. All the Melowies in the Winter Tower had coats and manes the color of winter, ice, and snow. Her bright-pink coat was completely out of place here. She really doubted that she could be from the Winter Realm.

"Well, here we are!" Mr. Zelus began. "Let's get started."

Everyone had dreamy looks in their eyes and smiles on their faces. Everyone except

Cleo, who was trying hard to keep her teeth from chattering.

"Don't worry too much about the cold, Cleo!" added the teacher with a grin. "Once we start our lesson, you will warm up! Let's get started right away with something that will help me see what level you are all at. I want everyone to make an ice cube. Visualize it as if it were in front of you, and voilà! Concentrate! "

Cleo tried to imagine an ice cube on the floor in front of her. She squinted her eyes, stuck out her tongue, tensed all her muscles, and

wrapped her wings around herself. But nothing happened. Absolutely nothing!

"Hey! Look at this!" cried Glenda, a little Melowy with a short mane and bangs, as she pointed to a piece of ice that had appeared near her front hooves. It looked more like a tiny, lumpy spike of ice than a cube, but at least it was something.

"Good job!" exclaimed Mr. Zelus.

Cleo squinted even more and concentrated as hard as she could, but instead of making ice, she accidentally bit her tongue. "Ouch!" she complained. "This is impossible!"

"For you, maybe, since you shouldn't even be here," said Eris as a little ice cube appeared in front of her. Well, it wasn't exactly a cube, but it was definitely ice.

"Well done!" Mr. Zelus exclaimed. He hadn't heard what Eris said to Cleo. But Cora heard, and it made her very upset. *How dare that ridiculous Melowy speak to my friend that way!* she thought. Suddenly, a perfect ice cube that glittered like a diamond appeared in front of Cora.

"Excellent!" Mr. Zelus beamed. "Absolutely excellent! The best ice cube I have ever seen at a first lesson." Cora returned Eris's angry glare with a pleasant smile.

Cleo had a difficult week. Every afternoon she went to a different tower and, she thought, made a complete fool of herself in different ways at each one.

In the Day Tower, she got sunburned on the tip of her muzzle but couldn't manage to make as much as a spark. Electra was able to start a wonderful little fire, which Ms. Diane had to quickly put out before someone burned their tail.

In the Spring Tower, Cleo got herself all tangled up in the climbing plants on the walls, and she wasn't able to make a single

sprout. Maya made a pretty little primrose appear out of thin air.

In the Night Tower, Cleo couldn't put out her candle no matter what she did, while Selena was able to do it after just three tries.

Cleo felt lower than ever and locked herself away in the library to study. She thought if she could find out more about the realms of Aura and the powers of the Melowies, she might be able to figure out which realm she was from. "I would like to check out *The History of the Realms and Their Powers*," she said to the librarian.

The pegasus with a lilac coat glared at her. "That is a second-year textbook, and if I am not mistaken, you are just a first-year student."

"Yes, but—"

"Just because Principal Gia was kind enough to take in a foundling like you doesn't mean you should be given any special treatment!"

As much as Cleo loved reading, she did not like the librarian, Ms. Circe. She always seemed to be trying to get rid of her, while Cleo would have loved to look through every book in the library one by one. "But there is no rule that says I can't read it," Cleo said quickly.

Ms. Circe snorted, walked over to a bookshelf, and took down a very big book. "Here," she said, handing the book to Cleo. "But you won't understand a thing."

Cleo bit her tongue to keep from making a wisecrack and flew straight to the reading room, carrying the big book. She sat down on one of the hanging sofas and buried her muzzle between the pages of the book.

Unfortunately, the book was just a list of boring dynasties and powers. She was about to give up when a line from the second-to-last page of the book made her jump up in her seat.

Such a power will not appear for many years—not until the arrival of a Melowy whose realm will be unknown.

Cleo dropped her bag in shock, sending her stuff scattering all over the floor. She turned to read the rest of the paragraph on the next page.

But the last page wasn't there. Someone had torn it out.

5
A Visit Home

"Cleo, my little cupcake!" a familiar voice called. "I knew I would find you here! You always have your muzzle in a book."

"Theodora!" Cleo cried. She put her book down and gave the school cook a big hug, burying her face in her vanilla-scented mane. Theodora was the pegasus who raised Cleo after Principal Gia found her on the front steps of the school. Cleo loved Theodora very much.

"Sorry that I haven't come to visit," Cleo said with a frown.

"Oh, that's okay, sweetie. You are busy with your classes and homework. And it's only fair that you get to spend some time with your friends. Remember, they can't just pop home to visit whenever they are feeling homesick."

"Speaking of feeling homesick . . . can I walk home with you?" Cleo asked, a little embarrassed.

"Of course you can! You're in luck. I just made some cookies," Theodora said with a wink. Cleo let herself be wrapped up in Theodora's warm hug and followed the cook out of the castle.

Home was just the same as it was when

she left: neat, colorful, and with a wonderful smell of vanilla, cocoa, and cinnamon floating in the air. Fluffy, Theodora's little dog, ran over to Cleo and started jumping excitedly around her. That day Fluffy had a big pink bow right in the middle of her head and was wearing a cute little white sweater.

"Now, tell me what's wrong," Theodora said, placing two cups of steaming tea and a plate of honey cookies on the table in front of Cleo.

"Well, it's just that we've started Art of Powers classes," explained

Cleo. She dunked a cookie in her tea while Fluffy got comfortable in her lap.

"You must be so tired!" Theodora exclaimed.

"Actually, I feel more sad than tired. I don't belong to any realm. I don't have a power," Cleo said.

"What gave you that idea?"

"I can't do anything!" Cleo said, then stuffed the cookie into her mouth. "The others can make ice cubes and flowers appear out of nowhere! They can light fires and put out candles!"

"And what have the teachers said about it?" Theodora asked.

"That I shouldn't give up and I just need to keep on trying until I figure out what my power is."

"So, don't you think you should do as you're told and keep trying?" Theodora said gently. "After all, they know better than you do. They are experts."

"You're right. But I am so afraid I will never figure it out. What if I can't? Will I be expelled?"

"But you will figure it out! Your mother knew that . . ."

Cleo jumped out of her chair, making sure Fluffy didn't go flying. She had been trying her hardest to steal a cookie from the table.

"My mother? You know who my mother is and you never told me?" Cleo said, almost shouting.

Theodora blushed and coughed, clearing her throat. "No, silly . . . I don't know her, or know who she is. I just mean, well, she left you on the steps of the Castle of Destiny. She must have known you belonged here, that it was the right place for you."

Cleo sat back down, taking a sip of her tea. Theodora had a good point. She had never thought of it that way.

"Maybe my mom was a Melowy and knew that I would be just like her."

"Exactly." Theodora nodded. "You just need to have more faith in yourself."

"You are right," Cleo said. "I should get going. I still have a lot of work to do for tomorrow."

"Here, take some cookies with you to share with your friends," said the cook, wrapping the leftover cookies up to go.

"I don't know if I can fit them in my bag." Cleo looked around, puzzled. "Hey, where is my bag?" She jumped up again, sending Fluffy sliding across the floor. She had left her bag in the library, and she was sure Ms. Circe wouldn't keep the library open a moment longer than usual. Especially not for her!

Cleo got to the library ten minutes after closing time. Luckily, though, the door was still open. When she went in, she saw Ms. Circe talking to Eris. "Here you will find every spell you need," Ms. Circe was saying, handing the Melowy a small book with a black cover.

"This will definitely make me the best in the class!" Eris said with an evil grin.

Cleo quickly hid behind a bookshelf. Eris was going to use the book to cheat in Art of Powers class, and Ms. Circe was helping her do it!

Cleo grabbed her bag quickly and quietly so that they would not see her. She'd never liked Ms. Circe, but she had no idea the librarian was so bad that she would encourage a student to cheat! Cleo wished she had not seen them, even though it was probably lucky that she did.

6
Rainbow Milk Shakes

"Now, who would like to try to create a snowflake?" Mr. Zelus asked. Worried whispers spread throughout the Winter Tower. Making a snowflake sounded a lot harder than the ice cube they'd had to make during their last lesson.

"I would like to try it!" Eris said, stepping forward. As she was walking to the front of the class, she bumped right into Cora.

"Hey, be careful!" Cora snapped.

"You should really learn to get out of people's way," Eris said with a nasty smile. "I didn't do it on purpose!"

But Cleo was sure she had because she also saw that Eris had shot a violet spark at her friend. *Did she cast a spell on Cora?* she wondered. *What if she turns into a statue? Or disappears?* But nothing happened.

Eris made a beautiful snowflake, and all of the other students clapped.

"Cora, would you like to try now?" the teacher asked.

"Sure." She trotted confidently up to the front of the class. She concentrated hard, and with all eyes on her, a piece of ice materialized at her hooves. But before anyone could clap for her, it melted, leaving nothing but a tiny puddle. Cora was surprised, and worried. It wasn't like her to fail so badly!

"I . . . I . . . I can't!" she admitted, her voice trembling like she was about to cry.

Eris chuckled.

"These things happen," said Mr. Zelus in an understanding tone. "You have only just started your lessons. Perhaps you didn't sleep very well last night? Are you sure you

had enough to eat for lunch? Using your power can take up a lot of energy, you know."

"Yes, sir."

"Maybe you are overworked. After all, you are the top of the class in so many subjects."

Cora smiled, glad that the teacher at least knew what a good student she was.

"Maybe," he continued, "you are even a little scared of your power. That does happen. I have seen the best of students go into a panic. Stick around after class and I will give you the recipe for a relaxing herbal tea and some breathing exercises that reduce stress."

*　　*　　*

Later that afternoon, Sugar and Spice, the café at the Castle of Destiny, was crowded with students. Cora and Cleo joined Maya, Electra, and Selena at their favorite table next to the window.

"Hello!" Maya said with a smile. "How was your day?"

"Terrible," said Cora coldly before falling silent.

Zoe, the owner of the café, rushed over to their table with her pencil and order pad. "It looks like someone here needs an apple, chamomile, and lime smoothie! That will

put a smile on your face again!" she said, pointing to Cora.

Just then, Cora spotted Eris staring at them from a few tables away, with an evil look in her eyes.

"I'm sorry, Zoe. I don't really want anything, but thank you," Cora said, getting up from the table. "I think I will go for a stroll around the garden. After being shut up in a classroom all afternoon, I need some fresh air."

Nothing like this had ever happened to Cora before. She was always top of the class in all of her subjects. What if her power just wasn't as strong as it needed to be? That was something even hard work wouldn't fix!

The cool air in the garden made her feel a little bit better. She passed Ben, the gardener, who was pruning a rosebush and mumbling to himself. Finally, she found a more private space and sat down. She took a deep breath and tried to do one of Mr. Zelus's breathing exercises to make herself feel better.

"Cora!" She turned to see Cleo coming toward her. "It isn't your fault. Your power works just fine. But then something happened and . . . ," she began to say, all at once.

"I know that you are trying to make me feel better, but you don't have to make excuses for me," Cora said.

"I am not making up excuses! There is more going on than you know! I saw Eris borrowing a book of magic spells from the library."

"A book of spells?" Cora repeated.

"Yes! Ms. Circe gave it to her. But if she had known that Eris was going to use it to cast a spell on you, I bet she never would have given it to her! She thought Eris wanted to study her own power. That evil Melowy even fooled the librarian!" Cleo explained. "It was no accident when she bumped into you in class. She put a spell on you!"

7

The Forbidden Book

"Today we are going to practice using our powers in a different environment," announced Mr. Zelus, trying to smooth out his sweater.

That day, class was near the waterfall in the garden. Cleo breathed a sigh of relief. At least she wasn't going to freeze! She was immediately distracted by the evil smirk on Eris's face.

Cora shook with rage. Eris had cheated. It was one thing to try to beat her by being the best in the class, but it was another thing to do it by cheating! She wasn't going to let Eris get away with it. But what could she do? She couldn't just accuse Eris without any proof.

"Please put your bags down. For this lesson, you will not need your books," said Mr. Zelus.

"We could look inside her bag," Cleo suggested to Cora. "Maybe she has the magic book in there."

"That would be wrong!" whispered Cora.

"Eris cast a spell on you, and you are still worried about your good manners," Cleo said, grinning.

Cora stuck out her chin with pride. "That

is why she will never be as good as me, and why she always has to use dirty tricks to get what she wants."

"I, however, do not have a problem doing it," Cleo continued. "If Eris has nothing to hide, then it won't matter if we take a peek, right?"

"Cleo!" said Cora, looking around.

"Hey, what are you doing?" Eris exclaimed, rushing over to them.

"I was just looking for a place to put my things," she answered, trying to sound normal. "Why do you want to know?"

Eris ignored her and moved her bag over. As she did, Cleo and Cora got a peek of what was inside.

"Did you see that?" whispered Cleo, excited. "A black book!"

"Yes, but what do we do now?" asked Cora.

The lesson was starting, and Mr. Zelus asked the students to create ice sculptures out of the water from the waterfall. Eris created something amazing, a life-sized pegasus. But no one else was doing very well. Glenda made a kind of icy butterfly, while her friend Irina

made an elf. It was a little lopsided, but still nice.

Cleo and Cora tried their best, but after an hour they still had not been able to make anything.

"Come on, you two!" Mr. Zelus called, coming over to them with a thermos. "Don't lose heart! Here is some of my calming herbal tea. It will make you feel better!"

Cora took a sip, trying not to make a face. Mr. Zelus was nice, but he had some really strange ideas.

"Let's try some stretching exercises to get rid of any stress on your shoulders," he continued. He demonstrated an exercise. "Put your tail down to the ground, raise your muzzle up to the sky, and streeeeetch your back!"

Cleo and Cora looked at him with puzzled expressions but did as they were told. They were already horribly embarrassed by not being able to make a sculpture; how much worse could this be?

"Oh, enough of this," Cora whispered. "I have to know what's in that bag!"

"What if Eris sees?" Cleo asked.

"The only other option is to fail."

Mr. Zelus was concentrating on explaining the exercise while Cleo backed up toward the bags. Eris, who was bragging to her friends about her ice sculpture, didn't notice what was happening until it was already too late.

The title of the book was *Increasing and Stealing Magic*. There was a big red stamp on the cover that said FORBIDDEN BOOK. Cleo was holding the book in her hooves, trotting over to show Mr. Zelus, when . . .

"Stop right there!" Eris yelled. Cleo dropped the book and screamed. All of a sudden, the book was locked in an ice sculpture in the shape of a pirate's treasure chest!

8
Cleo's Power

Cleo shook with anger. Eris could not get away with this! Cleo had to smash the chest! She had to show everyone the truth. Suddenly, a pink light began to form around her. It shot out from her horn like a laser beam and shattered the ice chest into a million pieces.

"Wow!" exclaimed Mr. Zelus as he trotted over to her. "So, that is your power. Very good. We now not only know that you have a power, but we also know that it is very strong. Of course, it is too soon to say which realm it comes from. The next time we meet, we will see how you create it and how you should use it. Until then, be very careful. Never use your power outside of the classroom. It could be dangerous if it is not used properly." Mr. Zelus picked up what remained of the forbidden book. It was basically confetti.

Eris smiled. The evidence against her had been destroyed. But her victory was short-lived. With a sudden crash, her pegasus sculpture shattered into pieces.

"Nooooo!" she shouted.

"The spell has been broken," Cora whispered to Cleo. "Thank you." The moment she said it, she felt her own power flooding back into her. A beautiful sculpture of a pegasus appeared in front of her. It was much more beautiful and detailed than the one Eris had made. The face even had a big smile on it. It was a sculpture of Cleo.

"Wow!" Cleo exclaimed, and she gave her friend a big hug. "It's so beautiful. I wish I could keep it in our dormitory!"

"Very good! I see that Cora has overcome whatever was blocking her magic," Mr. Zelus said, admiring the ice sculpture. "Of course, it's all because of my stretches and herbal tea. At the end of class I will pass along the steps and recipes to everyone. Best to do the stretches twice a day. Once in the morning and once at night. And you, Eris, don't lose heart. A lot of students start off with beginner's luck. All you need is some practice, and your power will grow in no time."

Eris shook her hooves in anger but did not dare argue. Cleo and Cora, on the other hand, enjoyed a round of applause from the whole class for finding their powers.

"So, we did it!" said Cora when they returned to their room in Butterfly Tower.

"Of course we did!" Cleo exclaimed. "I still don't really understand what it was I did, though."

"Little by little you will learn to use your power," said Cora. "You'll see. You can always count on me for help." She passed her friend a steaming cup of tea. "Would you like some?"

"Is it the same stuff Mr. Zelus made us drink?" Cleo said with a grin.

"No, it's an infusion of winter flowers. Back home, we drink it after long days to help us relax."

"I don't even know where my home is. I mean, it's always been the Castle of Destiny, but I don't know where I come from. It would be nice to have a home to return to one day."

"I know it isn't the same, but you are always welcome to come home with me for a visit!" Cora said, smiling. The two friends clinked their cups together and drank their tea. The friendship between them was growing stronger, and strong friendships don't really need a lot of words.

"There you are!" cried Electra, rushing into the room with Selena and Maya.

"You are going to have to tell us everything!" added Selena, sitting down next to Cora.

"We heard you found your power!" Maya said to Cleo.

The Melowy with the bright-pink mane looked at her roommates and smiled. She was so lucky to have such special friends.

The big, cold room in the Night Realm was lit by candles. The ruler and her two allies waited in silence for someone.

"Here I am, Your Immensity," said a hooded pegasus. Her footsteps echoed along the dark marble floor as she approached.

"Have you been able to test the Melowy we spoke about?" asked the ruler.

"Yes, and she proved worthy," she answered.

"Very good."

The hooded pegasus smiled a wicked smile.

See how it all began! Read the first exciting moment in the Melowies' journey:

Dreams Come True

The Big Day

Something very special was happening. Way up in the sky above the land of Aura, a magical trail had appeared in the clouds. It would only remain there for one day. Twenty-four pairs of wings fluttered in the cool air. Twenty-four silky manes sparkled in the morning light. Today was the big day. The day the Melowies were going to the Castle of Destiny for the first time!

Maya flapped her pink wings. She'd left

her home in the Spring Realm and was now flying with a bunch of other special pegasuses to the place they'd all dreamed about since they were little. She was so excited to finally find out more about her magic! It was just a shame that she was too shy to share her excitement with the others. But maybe, with a little effort . . .

Maya spotted a group of girls giggling nearby. She took a deep breath, flew over to them, and summoned her courage. "Hi, girls! How are you?" she whispered. The words were so soft that the others didn't hear. They glided away on a whistling air current without even noticing her.

Feeling disappointed, Maya watched them flying off into the distance. But then she noticed a pegasus with a purple mane who was floating all by herself. Maya flew over to her with a flutter of wings. "HELLO! WHAT'S YOUR NAME?" she said, this time far too loudly.

The stranger looked her up and down. In a flat voice, she answered, "Selena."

"I'm Maya. Umm . . . are you a Melowy, too?" Maya asked, trying to make conversation.

"Of course," the pretty pegasus replied.

Now Maya felt silly. Selena had to be a Melowy! Only Melowies, the pegasuses born with a symbol on their wings and a hidden magical power, could go where they were going.

EXPLORE DESTINY WITH THE MELOWIES AS THEY DISCOVER THEIR MAGICAL POWERS!

Hidden somewhere beyond the highest clouds is the Castle of Destiny, a school for very special students. They're the Melowies, young pegasuses born with a symbol on their wings and a hidden magical power. And the time destined for them to meet has now arrived.

scholastic.com

MELOWYe